The Drum
a folktale from India

There once was a poor woman who had only one child, a son. He was a good boy, always willing to help his mother out in any way he could. It was not an easy life, but they had each other, so the boy did not mind that his clothes were torn and he had few toys.

The boy had a secret wish. He had always wanted a drum.

One day when his mother was going to the village to sell some of their grain, she asked, "Is there anything you would like from the market?"

The boy thought and then said, "All I would really like, Mother, is a drum. I know you cannot get me one, but that is what I want most of all."

The boy was right. His mother knew she could not buy a drum. The grain that they grew and harvested to sell left only enough money to buy the few things she and her son could not make or grow themselves.

The poor woman thought of her son all the way home from the market, and was sad she could not get him the one thing that he really wanted.

She started to cry to herself as she walked home. Not seeing where she was going, she almost fell over a strange little man sitting by the side of the road.

"Why do you cry, good woman?" said the strange little man. The woman told him.

The strange little man gave the woman a piece of wood. "Maybe your boy would like this stick. It might have some magic in it," said the strange little man. "Perhaps my good son can find a use for it," she thought.

The boy did not know what to do with the stick when his mother gave it to him and told him what the strange little man said.

He thanked her and went out to play.

On the road the boy could see an old woman by a cook stove. The woman wanted to light a fire so she could cook bread. The wood was too new and would not catch fire.

Lots of smoke hung around her. Her eyes were wet and the boy asked her why she was crying. "I cannot get my fire to burn," said the woman.

"Here," said the boy, giving her his stick. "Perhaps this will help. My mother told me this stick has some magic in it. Maybe there is enough magic to start your fire."

The old woman started a fire. She thanked the boy, giving him some round, flat bread that she cooked on her stove.

The boy took the bread and walked on until he met another woman who was the wife of the village potter. A small child was in her arms, but the child was crying loudly and would not stop.

The boy spoke up so he could be heard. "Why is your child crying?" he asked.

The potter's wife answered, "He is hungry. We have nothing for him to eat." The boy looked at the bread he was holding in his hand, then gave it to the hungry child.

The child ate the bread and stopped crying at once. As thanks, the happy mother gave the boy a large pot.

The boy came to a river, where he found a man and a woman yelling. "Why all the yelling?" asked the boy.

"I am a washerman," the man replied. "And my wife has just broken the only pot I had to boil clothes in. I'll never get the clothing clean now."

The boy knew he could help the man and he gave them his pot. "Thank you very much," the washerman said, and he gave the boy a coat for being so nice.

The boy walked on until he came to a man with a horse on the road. The man wore sandals on his feet, and was only wearing underwear. His hair was wet and he was shivering.

The boy asked, "What happened to your clothes and why are you all wet?"

"I was on my way to visit my family when a robber rode up on this horse," the man replied. "He said I must give him my clothes and money. Then he pushed me in the river."

The boy handed the man the coat the washerman gave him. "Here." he said, "Put this on. It will keep you warm." The man put on the coat. "Please take this horse, I have no use for it," he told the boy.

The boy took the horse and kept walking down the road. He came to a wedding party made up of the bridegroom, his family, and some musicians with their instruments. But there was no music.

They were all seated in the shade of a small tree, and they looked very unhappy. "Why do you all look so sad?" the boy asked.

The father of the bridegroom spoke up. "We are waiting for the man who is bringing the horse my son will ride. He is very late and if my son cannot ride the horse during the wedding march, his marriage will have bad luck."

The boy listened to the story then gave the bridegroom his horse. "You saved the day!" the groom exclaimed.

The groom spoke to his father and one of the musicians. Then he handed the boy a drum. "Please take this drum, with all our thanks."

The boy's face lit up with joy. "Oh thank you, it is what I always wanted. Thank you so much, and may you have a wonderful wedding day."

The boy ran all the way home, as fast as he could go. He could not wait to show his mother that the strange little man was right.

That old piece of wood did have a little magic in it after all.